Become A Cyber Security Specialist

To become a cyber security specialist, it is important to have a strong foundation in computer science and programming.

Juwel Chowdhury

pencil

ISBN 978-93-5667-624-4
© Juwel Chowdhury 2023

Published in India 2023 by Pencil

A brand of
One Point Six Technologies Pvt. Ltd.
Unit no. 26, Ground Floor, Building A1,
Wadala Truck Terminal Road,
Near Post Office, Antop Hill, Mumbai - 400037
E connect@thepencilapp.com
W www.thepencilapp.com

DISCLAIMER: *This is a work of fiction. Names, characters, places, events and incidents are the products of the author's imagination. The opinions expressed in this book do not seek to reflect the views of the Publisher.*

Author biography

Juwel Chowdhury is a Computer Scientist, Cyber Security Specialist, internet personality, writer and YouTuber from Bangladesh.He also write previously book "Hackers Life". Juwel Chowdhury also working on movies. Juwel Chowdhury upload technology video on YouTube everyday. Juwel Chowdhury want told people about computer and computer science. He always try to help people about computer and computer science. Juwel Chowdhury loves computer and computer science also technology lots of. Juwel Chowdhury also writing more books about computer science.

CONTENTS

Chapter 1

To become a cyber security specialist, it is important to have a strong foundation in computer science and programming. This can be achieved through obtaining a degree in computer science or a related field, as well as hands-on experience with various programming languages. Additionally, having knowledge of networking, data structures and algorithms, operating systems, and cryptography is essential for a career in cyber security.

Certifications such as CompTIA Security+, Certified Ethical Hacker (CEH), and Certified Information Systems Security Professional (CISSP) can also demonstrate expertise and knowledge in the field.

Cyber security professionals should also stay updated on the latest technologies, trends and threats in the field by attending conferences, workshops, and participating in online communities. Networking with other professionals and specialists can also help to expand knowledge and build a strong professional network.

It is also important for cyber security specialists to adhere to ethical standards and laws related to the handling and protection of sensitive information. Specializing in a specific area of cyber security, such as network security, threat intelligence, or cloud security can increase career opportunities and earnings potential.

Finally, continuous learning is crucial in this rapidly evolving field. Cyber security professionals should always be looking to update their skills and knowledge through courses, attending conferences and workshops, and participating in research projects.

To become a cyber security specialist, consider the following steps:

Get an education: Pursue a degree in computer science, information security, or a related field.

Gain hands-on experience: Participate in cyber security-related projects and consider obtaining certifications such as CompTIA Security+, Certified Ethical Hacker (CEH), and Certified Information Systems Security Professional (CISSP).

Stay current: Stay updated on the latest technologies, trends and threats in cyber security by attending conferences, workshops, and participating in online communities.

Network: Connect with other cyber security professionals, both online and in-person, to expand your knowledge and learn about job opportunities.

Practice ethical behavior: Adhere to ethical standards, laws, and regulations related to cyber security.

Specialize: Consider specializing in a specific area of cyber security such as network security, threat intelligence, or cloud security.

Continuously learn: Cyber security is a constantly evolving field. Stay up-to-date by continuously learning and taking courses to maintain your skills and knowledge.

Build a strong portfolio: Document your work and projects, and create a portfolio that showcases your skills and knowledge in the field of cyber security.

Stay informed about industry developments: Stay informed about new technologies, trends, and threats in the field by reading industry publications, attending conferences and workshops, and participating in online communities.

Develop soft skills: In addition to technical skills, having strong communication, problem-solving, and leadership skills is important in the field of cyber security.

Participate in hackathons and competitions: Participating in hackathons and competitions can provide hands-on experience, build your skills, and demonstrate your abilities to potential employers.

Join a professional association: Consider joining a professional association, such as the International Association of Computer Security Professionals (ISC)², which can provide access to resources, training, and networking opportunities.

Consider obtaining additional certifications: Continuously obtaining additional certifications can demonstrate your dedication and commitment to the field, as well as keep your skills and knowledge up-to-date.

Engage in ethical hacking: Ethical hacking can help you understand the tactics, techniques, and procedures used by malicious hackers, and how to protect against them.

Get involved in research projects: Participating in research projects can provide opportunities to work with other experts in the field, learn about new technologies and techniques, and contribute to advancing the field of cyber security.

Collaborate with other departments: Cyber security is a collaborative effort that involves multiple departments within an organization. Building relationships and working with other departments can provide a better understanding of the organization's overall security posture.

Practice critical thinking: Being able to think critically, analyze problems, and come up with effective solutions is a crucial skill for cyber security specialists.

Build a network of mentors: Building a network of mentors who have experience in the field of cyber security can provide guidance, advice, and support as you progress in your career.

Be proactive: Take a proactive approach to cyber security by staying informed about the latest threats, testing your systems, and developing mitigation strategies.

Seek out opportunities for professional development: Continuously seeking out opportunities for professional development, such as attending conferences, workshops, and training programs, can help you stay current and advance your career in cyber security.

Have a strong attention to detail: In cyber security, attention to detail is crucial. Small mistakes can have major consequences, so it is important to be meticulous and precise in your work.

Familiarize yourself with security tools: Having a strong understanding of security tools such as firewalls, intrusion detection systems, and anti-virus software is important for cyber security specialists.

Be familiar with security regulations: Familiarize yourself with regulations such as HIPAA, PCI-DSS, and GDPR to ensure that you are adhering to industry standards and laws.

Develop a solid understanding of cryptography: Cryptography is a key component of cyber security, so it is important to have a solid understanding of encryption methods and how to secure communications.

Stay organized: Being organized and having a well-structured approach to your work is crucial in cyber security, as it helps to minimize errors and keep track of important information.

Collaborate with other security teams: Collaborating with other security teams can help to build a stronger, more comprehensive security posture for your organization.

Practice incident response: Prepare for potential security incidents by developing an incident response plan and regularly practicing incident response scenarios.

Never stop learning: Cyber security is a constantly evolving field, so it is important to never stop learning and to always be open to new ideas and technologies.

Communicate effectively: Effective communication is crucial in cyber security, both for explaining technical concepts to non-technical stakeholders and for collaborating with other security teams.

Be proactive in identifying threats: Be proactive in identifying and mitigating potential threats by regularly monitoring systems, staying informed about the latest threats, and conducting security audits.

Develop a risk management plan: Develop a comprehensive risk management plan that identifies potential threats, assesses their impact, and outlines mitigation strategies.

Know your organization's infrastructure: Having a thorough understanding of your organization's infrastructure and how it functions is essential for identifying potential security weaknesses and implementing effective security measures.

Be aware of social engineering tactics: Be aware of social engineering tactics, such as phishing and pretexting, and educate your colleagues and stakeholders about these tactics.

Continuously assess and improve security measures: Continuously assess and improve your organization's security measures to ensure that they are effective and up-to-date.

Build relationships with vendors: Building strong relationships with vendors and partners can help to ensure that security measures are implemented effectively and efficiently.

Participate in penetration testing: Regularly participate in penetration testing to identify potential security weaknesses and to validate the effectiveness of security measures.

Stay up-to-date with industry developments: Regularly staying informed about new technologies, threats, and industry developments can help you stay ahead of potential security risks and make informed decisions about security measures.

Encourage a security-conscious culture: Encourage a security-conscious culture within your organization by educating stakeholders, promoting security best practices, and setting a positive example.

Foster a culture of continuous improvement: Foster a culture of continuous improvement by regularly reassessing security measures, seeking out opportunities for professional development, and continuously seeking to improve security processes and protocols.

Practice data privacy: Ensure that sensitive data is protected by following privacy laws and regulations, using encryption, and limiting access to sensitive data.

Prepare for disaster recovery: Prepare for potential security incidents by developing a disaster recovery plan, regularly backing up data, and testing disaster recovery processes.

Participate in threat intelligence sharing: Participate in threat intelligence sharing programs and communities to stay informed about emerging threats and to collaborate with other security professionals.

Be prepared to respond to security incidents: Be prepared to respond quickly and effectively to security incidents by having a well-defined incident response plan and regularly practicing incident response scenarios.

Encourage regular software updates: Encourage regular software updates to ensure that systems are protected from known vulnerabilities and to stay current with security patches.

Implement access controls: Implement access controls, such as passwords and two-factor authentication, to limit unauthorized access to sensitive data and systems.

Conduct regular security audits: Conduct regular security audits to identify potential security weaknesses and to ensure that security measures are functioning as intended.

Promote secure software development practices: Promote secure software development practices, such as threat modeling and code review, to ensure that applications are secure from the outset.

Educate stakeholders about cyber security: Educate stakeholders about the importance of cyber security and best practices for protecting sensitive data and systems.

Develop secure configurations: Develop secure configurations for systems and networks to minimize potential security risks and to ensure that systems are configured to meet security requirements.

Partner with security vendors: Partner with security vendors to gain access to the latest security tools and technologies, and to ensure that security measures are integrated effectively.

Regularly evaluate security measures: Regularly evaluate security measures to ensure that they are effective, efficient, and aligned with the needs of the organization.

Foster a culture of continuous learning: Foster a culture of continuous learning by seeking out opportunities for professional development, attending industry conferences, and continuously seeking to expand your knowledge and skills.

Implement strong passwords: Implement strong passwords and encourage employees to do the same, to reduce the risk of unauthorized access to sensitive information.

Train employees: Train employees on security policies, procedures and best practices, to ensure that everyone is aware of their role in maintaining the security of the organization.

Monitor and review logs: Regularly monitor and review logs to identify any unusual activity, and take appropriate action to prevent potential security incidents.

Encrypt sensitive data: Encrypt sensitive data to protect it from unauthorized access, both in transit and at rest.

Conduct regular risk assessments: Conduct regular risk assessments to identify and prioritize potential security threats and vulnerabilities.

Implement access controls: Implement access controls to limit who can access sensitive information and resources, based on their role and responsibility within the organization.

Use firewalls: Use firewalls to block unauthorized access to the network and prevent cyber attacks.

Update software and systems: Regularly update software and systems to ensure that they are protected against known vulnerabilities and threats.

Dispose of data securely: Dispose of data securely, using secure methods to prevent unauthorized access to sensitive information.

Keep software licenses up to date: Keep software licenses up to date to ensure that you are using the most secure and up-to-date versions of software and systems.

Use multi-factor authentication: Use multi-factor authentication to provide an extra layer of security for sensitive information and systems.

Conduct regular backups: Conduct regular backups of sensitive data and systems, to minimize the impact of any security incidents or data loss.

Restrict physical access: Restrict physical access to sensitive information and systems, to prevent unauthorized access or theft.

Have a disaster recovery plan: Have a disaster recovery plan in place, to ensure that the organization can quickly respond to and recover from any security incidents or data loss.

Have a security incident response plan: Have a security incident response plan in place, to ensure that the organization is prepared to respond to and manage security incidents effectively.

Monitor network traffic: Monitor network traffic to identify any suspicious activity and prevent potential security incidents.

Educate employees on phishing: Educate employees on how to identify and avoid phishing attacks, to reduce the risk of sensitive information being compromised.

Use anti-virus software: Use anti-virus software to protect against malware and other malicious software that can compromise the security of the organization.

Implement data loss prevention: Implement data loss prevention (DLP) measures to detect and prevent the unauthorized sharing or exfiltration of sensitive information.

Use software patches: Use software patches to address vulnerabilities and protect systems against potential security threats.

Conduct penetration testing: Conduct penetration testing to identify and address potential security vulnerabilities in systems and applications.

Have an incident response team: Have an incident response team in place, to ensure that security incidents are managed quickly and effectively.

Use strong encryption for data transmission: Use strong encryption for data transmission, to protect sensitive information from interception and theft during transit.

Control the use of removable media: Control the use of removable media, such as USB drives and external hard drives, to prevent sensitive information from being stolen or lost.

Monitor third-party vendors: Monitor third-party vendors who have access to sensitive information, to ensure that their security practices are adequate and that sensitive information is protected.

Educate employees on safe online practices: Educate employees on safe online practices, such as avoiding public

Wi-Fi, using strong passwords, and verifying the legitimacy of emails and links.

Use a virtual private network (VPN): Use a virtual private network (VPN) to encrypt internet traffic and protect sensitive information during remote access.

Implement security awareness training: Implement security awareness training, to educate employees on how to identify and avoid potential security threats and vulnerabilities.

Limit administrative privileges: Limit administrative privileges to only those employees who need them, to reduce the risk of unauthorized access or changes to sensitive systems and data.

Use network segmentation: Use network segmentation to separate sensitive systems and data from less secure systems, to reduce the risk of compromise.

Ensure data privacy: Ensure data privacy by protecting sensitive information from unauthorized access, use, or disclosure.

Conduct security audits: Conduct security audits to identify any gaps in the organization's security posture and take action to address them.

Monitor and limit user activity: Monitor and limit user activity, to detect and prevent any suspicious or unauthorized activity on systems and data.

Use secure development practices: Use secure development practices, such as code reviews and penetration testing, to ensure that applications are secure and free from vulnerabilities.

Implement security by design: Implement security by design, considering security from the outset of projects and embedding it into processes and systems.

Use secure configurations: Use secure configurations for systems and software, to prevent potential security vulnerabilities.

Regularly test disaster recovery plans: Regularly test disaster recovery plans, to ensure that they are effective and can be quickly activated in the event of a security incident or data loss.

Have a clear security policy: Have a clear security policy, outlining the security measures in place and the responsibilities of employees, to ensure that everyone understands the importance of security and their role in maintaining it.

Monitor for potential threats: Monitor for potential threats, such as cyber attacks, malware, and data breaches, to quickly detect and respond to any incidents.

Implement access controls: Implement access controls, such as passwords, biometrics, and multi-factor authentication, to prevent unauthorized access to systems and data.

Use secure file storage: Use secure file storage, such as encrypted cloud storage, to protect sensitive information from unauthorized access.

Ensure software licensing compliance: Ensure software licensing compliance, to avoid any legal issues or fines related to unlicensed software use.

Train employees on privacy laws: Train employees on privacy laws, such as GDPR and HIPAA, to ensure that sensitive information is protected and handled in accordance with regulations.

Use firewalls: Use firewalls to protect against network-based attacks and unauthorized access to systems.

Implement network security: Implement network security, such as firewalls, intrusion detection systems, and Virtual Private Networks, to protect against potential threats.

Encrypt sensitive data: Encrypt sensitive data, both in storage and in transit, to protect against unauthorized access or theft.

Perform regular risk assessments: Perform regular risk assessments, to identify potential threats and vulnerabilities and take action to address them.

Continuously evaluate and improve security measures: Continuously evaluate and improve security measures, to ensure that the organization is always protected against potential security threats.

All subject Analyze each example :

Regularly evaluate security measures: This statement highlights the importance of regularly reviewing and assessing the effectiveness of an organization's security measures. This is important to ensure that they are adequate and aligned with the needs of the organization, and to make any necessary changes to improve the overall security posture.

Foster a culture of continuous learning: This statement emphasizes the importance of professional development and continuous learning for employees in the field of security. By seeking out opportunities for growth and improvement, employees can stay up to date with the latest security practices and technologies, which can help to ensure the overall security of the organization.

Implement data loss prevention: Data loss prevention is a critical aspect of security that helps to prevent sensitive information from being lost or stolen. By implementing DLP measures, organizations can ensure that sensitive data is protected and that any incidents are quickly detected and addressed.

Use software patches: Regular software patches help to address vulnerabilities in systems and applications, which can reduce the risk of potential security threats. By using software patches, organizations can ensure that their systems and data are protected against potential attacks.

Conduct penetration testing: Penetration testing is a valuable tool for identifying potential security vulnerabilities in systems and applications. By conducting these tests, organizations can identify any weaknesses and take action to address them, which can help to improve the overall security posture of the organization.

Have an incident response team: An incident response team is critical in managing security incidents quickly and effectively. By having a dedicated team in place, organizations can respond to incidents in a timely manner, which can help to minimize the impact of any security incidents.

Implement security awareness training: Security awareness training is important for educating employees on safe online practices and identifying potential security threats. By implementing this training, organizations can improve employee understanding of security and help to reduce the risk of security incidents.

Monitor for potential threats: This statement emphasizes the importance of ongoing monitoring for potential security threats, such as cyber attacks, malware, and data breaches. By monitoring for potential threats, organizations can quickly detect and respond to any incidents, which can help to minimize the impact and damage of a security breach.

Implement access controls: Access controls, such as passwords, biometrics, and multi-factor authentication, are important measures to prevent unauthorized access to systems and data. By implementing these controls, organizations can help to ensure that sensitive information is protected from potential threats.

Use secure file storage: Secure file storage, such as encrypted cloud storage, helps to protect sensitive information from unauthorized access. By using secure file storage, organizations can ensure that their data is protected and that any incidents are quickly detected and addressed.

Ensure software licensing compliance: This statement highlights the importance of ensuring that all software used by an organization is properly licensed. By doing so, organizations can avoid any legal issues or fines related to unlicensed software use, which can help to protect their reputation and credibility.

Train employees on privacy laws: Privacy laws, such as GDPR and HIPAA, play an important role in protecting sensitive information. By training employees on these laws, organizations can ensure that their employees are handling sensitive information in accordance with regulations, which can help to reduce the risk of security incidents.

Use firewalls: Firewalls play an important role in protecting against network-based attacks and unauthorized access to systems. By using firewalls, organizations can help to prevent potential security threats and improve the overall security posture of their systems.

Implement network security: Network security, such as firewalls, intrusion detection systems, and Virtual Private Networks, helps to protect against potential security threats. By implementing these measures, organizations can improve the overall security of their network and reduce the risk of security incidents.

Encrypt sensitive data: Encryption helps to protect sensitive information from unauthorized access or theft. By encrypting sensitive data, both in storage and in transit, organizations can help to ensure that their data is protected and that any incidents are quickly detected and addressed.

Perform regular risk assessments: Regular risk assessments help organizations to identify potential security threats and vulnerabilities, and take action to address them. By performing regular risk assessments, organizations can improve their overall security posture and reduce the risk of security incidents.

Continuously evaluate and improve security measures: This statement emphasizes the importance of continuously evaluating and improving security measures to ensure that an organization is always protected against potential security threats. By continuously evaluating and improving security measures, organizations can stay ahead of potential threats and improve their overall security posture.

Cybersecurity is an important aspect of today's digital world. As technology advances, the threat of cyber attacks and security breaches increases. Organizations must take steps to ensure the protection of their systems, applications, and sensitive data from potential threats. In this essay, we will discuss 10 essential security measures that organizations should implement to improve their overall security posture.

Regularly evaluate security measures: Organizations must regularly review and assess the effectiveness of their security measures to ensure that they are adequate and aligned with the needs of the organization. This can involve conducting regular risk assessments, penetration testing, and security audits to identify potential vulnerabilities and take action to address them.

Foster a culture of continuous learning: By seeking out opportunities for professional development and continuous learning, organizations can ensure that their employees are up to date with the latest security practices and technologies. This can involve attending industry conferences, taking online courses, and regularly seeking out new information and skills in the field of cybersecurity.

Implement data loss prevention: Data loss prevention is a critical aspect of security that helps to prevent sensitive information from being lost or stolen. This can involve implementing measures such as encryption, secure file storage, and access controls to ensure that sensitive data is protected and that any incidents are quickly detected and addressed.

Use software patches: Regular software patches help to address vulnerabilities in systems and applications, which can reduce the risk of potential security threats. By keeping systems and applications up to date, organizations can ensure that their systems and data are protected against potential attacks.

Conduct penetration testing: Penetration testing is a valuable tool for identifying potential security vulnerabilities in systems and applications. By conducting these tests, organizations can identify any weaknesses and take action to address them, which can help to improve the overall security posture of the organization.

Have an incident response team: An incident response team is critical in managing security incidents quickly and effectively. By having a dedicated team in place, organizations can respond to incidents in a timely manner, which can help to minimize the impact of any security incidents.

Implement security awareness training: Security awareness training is important for educating employees on safe online practices and identifying potential security threats. By implementing this training, organizations can improve employee understanding of security and help to reduce the risk of security incidents.

Monitor for potential threats: Ongoing monitoring for potential security threats, such as cyber attacks, malware, and data breaches, is essential for quickly detecting and responding to any incidents. By monitoring for potential threats, organizations can minimize the impact and damage of a security breach.

Implement access controls: Access controls, such as passwords, biometrics, and multi-factor authentication, are important measures to prevent unauthorized access to systems and data. By implementing these controls, organizations can help to ensure that sensitive information is protected from potential threats.

Use firewalls: Firewalls play an important role in protecting against network-based attacks and unauthorized access to systems. By using firewalls, organizations can help to prevent potential security threats and improve the overall security posture of their systems.

In conclusion, cybersecurity is an essential aspect of today's digital world. Organizations must take steps to ensure the protection of their systems, applications, and sensitive data from potential threats. By implementing measures such as regular security evaluations, a culture of continuous learning, data loss prevention, software patches, penetration testing, incident response teams, security awareness training, monitoring for potential threats, access controls, and firewalls, organizations can improve their overall security posture and reduce the risk of security incidents.

Regular security evaluations: Regularly reviewing and assessing the effectiveness of an organization's security measures is crucial to ensure that they are adequate and aligned with the needs of the organization. This can involve conducting regular risk assessments, penetration testing, and security audits to identify potential vulnerabilities and take action to address them.

Culture of continuous learning: By fostering a culture of continuous learning, organizations can ensure that their employees are up to date with the latest security practices and technologies. This can involve attending industry conferences, taking online courses, and regularly seeking out new information and skills in the field of cybersecurity.

Data loss prevention: Data loss prevention helps to prevent sensitive information from being lost or stolen and can involve implementing measures such as encryption, secure file storage, and access controls.

Software patches: Regular software patches help address vulnerabilities in systems and applications and reduce the risk of potential security threats. By keeping systems and applications up to date, organizations can improve their security posture.

Incident response teams: An incident response team is critical in managing security incidents quickly and effectively. By having a dedicated team in place, organizations can respond to incidents in a timely manner, which can help minimize the impact of any security incidents.

Cybersecurity is a critical aspect of any organization today. With the increasing reliance on technology and the internet, the threat of cyber attacks has become a major concern for businesses of all sizes. As such, it is essential for organizations to take proactive measures to protect their systems, data, and sensitive information from potential threats. In this essay, we will discuss five key steps that organizations can take to improve their cybersecurity posture.

The first step that organizations can take to improve their cybersecurity is to regularly evaluate their security measures. Regular security evaluations can help organizations identify potential vulnerabilities in their systems and take action to address them. This can involve conducting regular risk assessments, penetration testing, and security audits. By regularly reviewing their security measures, organizations can ensure that they are effective, efficient, and aligned with their needs. For example, an organization might find that their firewalls are outdated or that their employees are not adequately trained on the latest security practices. In such cases, the organization can take steps to address these issues and improve their security posture.

Another important aspect of cybersecurity is fostering a culture of continuous learning. With the fast pace of technological advancement, it is essential for organizations to ensure that their employees are up to date with the latest security practices and technologies. By fostering a culture of continuous learning, organizations can encourage their employees to seek out opportunities for professional development, attend industry conferences, and continuously expand their knowledge and skills. For example, organizations can invest in online security courses or send their employees to cybersecurity conferences to gain new insights into the latest trends and best practices.

Data loss prevention is another critical aspect of cybersecurity. With the growing volume of sensitive information being stored electronically, it is essential for organizations to take measures to prevent data loss. Data loss prevention involves implementing measures such as encryption, secure file storage, and access controls to protect sensitive information from being lost or stolen. For example, an organization might choose to store sensitive data on an encrypted server or use multi-factor authentication to ensure that only authorized personnel have access to sensitive information. By taking steps to prevent data loss, organizations can minimize the risk of potential security incidents and ensure the privacy and security of their data.

Software patches are an important aspect of cybersecurity that organizations cannot afford to ignore. Regular software patches help address vulnerabilities in systems and applications and reduce the risk of potential security threats. By keeping their systems and applications up to date, organizations can improve their security posture and reduce the risk of potential threats. For example, if a vulnerability is discovered in a popular software application, the vendor might release a patch to address the vulnerability. By applying the patch, organizations can protect themselves from potential threats and reduce their risk of being affected by a cyber attack.

Finally, incident response teams are a critical component of any organization's cybersecurity strategy. An incident response team is a dedicated group of individuals who are trained to manage security incidents quickly and effectively. By having a dedicated team in place, organizations can respond to incidents in a timely manner, which can help minimize the impact of any security incidents. For example, if a security breach occurs, the incident response team can work to contain the breach, identify the cause, and take steps to prevent similar incidents from occurring in the future.

In conclusion, cybersecurity is a critical aspect of any organization today. With the increasing threat of cyber attacks, it is essential for organizations to take proactive measures to protect their systems, data, and sensitive information. By regularly evaluating their security measures, fostering a culture of continuous learning, implementing data loss prevention measures, keeping software up to date, and having a dedicated incident response team, organizations can improve their cybersecurity posture and reduce the risk of potential threats.

Additionally, it is crucial for organizations to educate their employees about the importance of cybersecurity and the role they play in protecting sensitive information. Regular training sessions and workshops can help employees understand the importance of cyber hygiene and the role they play in maintaining the security of the organization. Employees should be trained on topics such as password management, email security, and avoiding phishing scams. By educating employees, organizations can help reduce the risk of security incidents and ensure that everyone is aware of the best practices to follow to maintain the security of the organization.

Organizations should also consider investing in security solutions and technologies to help improve their cybersecurity posture. This can include firewalls, antivirus software, intrusion detection systems, and security information and event management (SIEM) solutions. These solutions can help organizations detect and prevent potential threats in real-time and respond quickly to any incidents that do occur. By investing in security solutions, organizations can improve their visibility into their security posture, detect potential threats early, and respond quickly to incidents when they do occur.

Finally, it is crucial for organizations to have a comprehensive cybersecurity plan in place. A cybersecurity plan should outline the steps that organizations will take in the event of a security incident, including how they will respond, recover, and return to normal operations. The plan should also outline the roles and responsibilities of each individual within the organization and the procedures that they should follow in the event of a security incident. By having a comprehensive cybersecurity plan in place, organizations can ensure that they are prepared for potential security incidents and can respond quickly and effectively to minimize the impact of any incidents that do occur.

In conclusion, organizations need to take a comprehensive approach to cybersecurity to ensure the protection of their systems, data, and sensitive information. By regularly evaluating their security measures, fostering a culture of continuous learning, implementing data loss prevention measures, keeping software up to date, having a dedicated incident response team, and investing in security solutions, organizations can improve their cybersecurity posture and reduce the risk of potential threats. Additionally, by educating employees and having a comprehensive cybersecurity plan in place, organizations can ensure that they are prepared to respond quickly and effectively in the event of a security incident.

For organizations that rely heavily on technology and data, coding can play a significant role in enhancing their cybersecurity posture. Here are a few examples of how coding can be used to improve cybersecurity:

Implementing encryption: Encryption is a process that converts plain text into coded text to protect sensitive information from unauthorized access. In coding, encryption algorithms can be implemented to encrypt sensitive data at rest or in transit, making it much more difficult for malicious actors to access it. For example, in Python, the cryptography library can be used to implement encryption algorithms, such as AES (Advanced Encryption Standard) and RSA (Rivest-Shamir-Adleman).

Developing secure software: Software developers can write secure code by following best practices, such as input validation and error handling, to prevent potential vulnerabilities that could be exploited by attackers. For example, in Python, the OWASP (Open Web Application Security Project) has a number of resources that developers can use to learn about writing secure code.

Creating intrusion detection systems: Intrusion detection systems are used to detect and alert organizations of potential security incidents, such as unauthorized access or data breaches. In coding, intrusion detection systems can be developed using machine learning algorithms to analyze network traffic and identify unusual or malicious activity. For example, in Python, the scikit-learn library can be used to build machine learning algorithms for intrusion detection systems.

Building firewalls: Firewalls are used to protect networks from unauthorized access and can be developed using code. For example, in Python, the Scapy library can be used to build custom firewalls that can inspect network traffic and block malicious traffic before it reaches its destination.

Automating incident response: Organizations can use code to automate their incident response process, making it quicker and more efficient. For example, in Python, the Selenium library can be used to automate the process of logging into systems, retrieving logs, and performing other tasks that would otherwise need to be done manually in the event of a security incident.

In conclusion, coding can play a crucial role in enhancing an organization's cybersecurity posture. By implementing encryption, developing secure software, creating intrusion detection systems, building firewalls, and automating incident response, organizations can improve their security posture and reduce the risk of potential threats.

Additionally, there are several other ways that coding can help organizations improve their cybersecurity posture. For example:

Pen-testing: Penetration testing, also known as pen-testing, is a process used to identify vulnerabilities in systems and applications. In coding, pen-testing tools can be developed to automate the process of identifying and exploiting vulnerabilities, which can be used to test the security of a network or application. For example, in Python, the

Metasploit Framework can be used to automate pen-testing tasks.

Monitoring: Organizations can use code to automate the process of monitoring their systems and applications for potential security threats. For example, in Python, the Logstash library can be used to collect and analyze log data, which can be used to detect potential security incidents.

Developing intrusion prevention systems: Intrusion prevention systems are used to prevent security incidents by blocking malicious traffic before it reaches its destination. In coding, intrusion prevention systems can be developed using machine learning algorithms to analyze network traffic and identify potential security threats. For example, in Python, the TensorFlow library can be used to build machine learning algorithms for intrusion prevention systems.

Securing data: Organizations can use code to secure their data, such as by implementing access controls, encryption, and backup and recovery procedures. For example, in Python, the Django library can be used to build secure web applications that implement access controls and encryption for sensitive data.

Enhancing threat intelligence: Threat intelligence is information about potential security threats that organizations can use to improve their security posture. In coding, organizations can develop tools to automate the process of gathering, analyzing, and using threat intelligence data. For example, in Python, the Open Threat Exchange (OTX) library can be used to gather and analyze threat intelligence data.

In conclusion, coding plays a critical role in enhancing an organization's cybersecurity posture. By implementing encryption, developing secure software, creating intrusion detection and prevention systems, monitoring systems, securing data, and enhancing threat intelligence, organizations can improve their security posture and reduce the risk of potential threats. By investing in the development of coding skills, organizations can better prepare themselves for the rapidly evolving cybersecurity landscape.

Explain the above ten examples :

Encryption: Encryption is the process of encoding data to prevent unauthorized access. In coding, encryption algorithms can be developed to secure sensitive information, such as passwords, financial information, and personal data. For example, in Python, the PyCryptodome library can be used to encrypt and decrypt data.

Secure software development: Secure software development involves implementing security measures during the development process to prevent potential security threats. In coding, secure software development practices, such as input validation, access controls, and error handling, can be built into the code to prevent potential security incidents. For example, in Python, the OWASP Top 10 Project provides a list of the most critical security risks and recommendations for secure software development.

Intrusion detection and prevention: Intrusion detection systems are used to detect potential security incidents, while intrusion prevention systems are used to prevent them. In coding, intrusion detection and prevention systems can be developed to monitor network traffic and identify potential security threats. For example, in Python, the Suricata network security monitoring tool can be used to detect and prevent potential security incidents.

Monitoring: Monitoring systems are used to monitor networks and applications for potential security threats. In coding, monitoring systems can be developed to automate the process of collecting and analyzing log data, which can be used to detect potential security incidents. For example, in Python, the ELK stack, which consists of Elasticsearch, Logstash, and Kibana, can be used to monitor systems for potential security threats.

Access controls: Access controls are used to restrict access to sensitive information. In coding, access controls can be implemented to prevent unauthorized access to sensitive information. For example, in Python, the Django web framework provides built-in access controls that can be used to restrict access to sensitive information.

Cybersecurity is an ever-growing concern in today's digital world. As organizations increasingly rely on technology and store sensitive information online, it is imperative that they implement effective security measures to protect their systems, data, and customers. The following five topics are critical to building and maintaining a secure environment.

Encryption: Encryption is the process of encoding data to prevent unauthorized access. In coding, encryption algorithms can be developed to secure sensitive information, such as passwords, financial information, and personal data. For example, encryption can be used to secure data in transit, such as when transmitting sensitive information over the internet. By encrypting data, even if it is intercepted, it will be unreadable to anyone without the key to decrypt it.

Secure software development: Secure software development involves implementing security measures during the development process to prevent potential security threats. In coding, secure software development practices, such as input validation, access controls, and error handling, can be built into the code to prevent potential security incidents. For example, developers can implement secure coding practices to prevent SQL injection attacks, which allow attackers to execute malicious code by exploiting vulnerabilities in the database. By implementing secure software development practices, organizations can reduce the risk of potential security incidents.

Intrusion detection and prevention: Intrusion detection systems are used to detect potential security incidents, while intrusion prevention systems are used to prevent them. In coding, intrusion detection and prevention systems can be developed to monitor network traffic and identify potential security threats. For example, intrusion detection systems can be used to monitor network traffic for signs of suspicious activity, such as a sudden increase in traffic from a specific IP address. If a potential security incident is detected, the intrusion prevention system can take action, such as blocking the traffic or alerting the security team.

Monitoring: Monitoring systems are used to monitor networks and applications for potential security threats. In coding, monitoring systems can be developed to automate the process of collecting and analyzing log data, which can be used to detect potential security incidents. For example, monitoring systems can be used to track changes in the network and identify unusual patterns of behavior, such as a sudden spike in network traffic or a change in user activity. By continuously monitoring the network, organizations can quickly detect and respond to potential security incidents.

Access controls: Access controls are used to restrict access to sensitive information. In coding, access controls can be implemented to prevent unauthorized access to sensitive information. For example, access controls can be used to restrict access to sensitive information, such as confidential company data or personal information. By implementing access controls, organizations can ensure that only authorized personnel have access to sensitive information, reducing the risk of potential security incidents.

In conclusion, effective cybersecurity requires a combination of strong encryption, secure software development, intrusion detection and prevention, monitoring, and access controls. By implementing these measures, organizations can reduce the risk of potential security incidents and protect their systems, data, and customers. Additionally, it is important for organizations to stay up-to-date on the latest threats and vulnerabilities and continuously evaluate their security measures to ensure that they are effective, efficient, and aligned with the needs of the organization.

Moreover, fostering a culture of continuous learning is crucial in maintaining a secure environment. This involves seeking out opportunities for professional development, attending industry conferences, and continuously seeking to expand knowledge and skills. Staying informed of the latest developments in cybersecurity and taking advantage of training opportunities helps ensure that organizations have the knowledge and skills necessary to prevent and respond to potential security incidents.

In addition, regular audits and assessments can help organizations identify potential vulnerabilities and implement the necessary changes to strengthen their security measures. These assessments can include penetration testing, which involves simulating an attack on the network to identify potential vulnerabilities, and security assessments, which involve reviewing the organization's security measures and processes to identify potential weaknesses.

It is also important for organizations to have a well-defined incident response plan in place. This plan should include steps for responding to potential security incidents, such as how to contain the incident, how to prevent further damage, and how to recover from the incident. Having a well-defined incident response plan in place helps organizations respond quickly and effectively to potential security incidents and reduces the impact of the incident.

In conclusion, cybersecurity is a critical concern for organizations in today's digital world. By implementing strong security measures, fostering a culture of continuous learning, regularly assessing security measures, and having a well-defined incident response plan in place, organizations can reduce the risk of potential security incidents and protect their systems, data, and customers.

Additionally, it is important for organizations to implement and regularly update their access control policies. Access control policies define who has access to sensitive information and systems and under what circumstances they can access it. This helps to prevent unauthorized access and reduces the risk of data breaches. Another important aspect of cybersecurity is encryption.

Encrypting sensitive information helps to protect it from unauthorized access, even if the data is intercepted. This is particularly important for organizations that store and transmit sensitive information, such as financial information and personal data.

It is also important for organizations to implement and regularly update their backup and disaster recovery plans. This involves regularly backing up data and having a plan in place for how to recover data in the event of a disaster, such as a natural disaster or a cyber attack. This helps organizations ensure that they can recover from potential security incidents and minimize the impact of the incident.

Moreover, implementing multi-factor authentication can help to reduce the risk of unauthorized access to systems and data. Multi-factor authentication requires users to provide multiple forms of identification, such as a password and a security token, in order to access systems and data. This helps to prevent unauthorized access and reduces the risk of data breaches.

Finally, organizations should educate employees on good cybersecurity practices. This includes educating employees on the importance of strong passwords, avoiding phishing scams, and being vigilant when it comes to potential security incidents. This helps to reduce the risk of security incidents caused by human error and ensures that employees are aware of the steps they can take to help protect the organization's systems and data.

In conclusion, cybersecurity is a complex and ever-evolving issue that requires organizations to be proactive in their approach. By implementing strong security measures, fostering a culture of continuous learning, regularly assessing security measures, and having a well-defined incident response plan in place, organizations can reduce the risk of potential security incidents and protect their systems, data, and customers.

Additionally, it is important for organizations to regularly update their software and systems. Software and system vulnerabilities can be exploited by attackers to gain unauthorized access to systems and data. Regular software and system updates help to close these vulnerabilities and reduce the risk of security incidents.

Another important aspect of cybersecurity is monitoring and logging. Monitoring systems and logging activities help organizations detect potential security incidents and respond quickly. This includes monitoring systems for unusual activity, such as increased network traffic or unusual login attempts, and logging user activities to track who accessed sensitive information and when.

It is also important for organizations to implement a risk management framework. This framework should include identifying potential risks, assessing the likelihood and impact of these risks, and implementing controls to mitigate the risks. This helps organizations to prioritize their efforts and allocate resources to the areas that pose the greatest risk to their systems and data.

Moreover, organizations should consider implementing a security information and event management (SIEM) system. A SIEM system aggregates and analyzes security-related data from multiple sources, such as firewalls, intrusion detection systems, and endpoints. This helps organizations to detect and respond to potential security incidents more quickly and effectively.

Finally, organizations should be proactive in their approach to cybersecurity and work with their stakeholders, including customers, partners, and suppliers, to ensure the security of their systems and data. This includes working with stakeholders to implement strong security measures, sharing information about potential security threats, and working together to prevent and respond to security incidents.

In conclusion, cybersecurity is a critical concern for organizations in today's digital world. By being proactive in their approach to cybersecurity, implementing strong security measures, fostering a culture of continuous learning, regularly assessing security measures, and having a well-defined incident response plan in place, organizations can reduce the risk of potential security incidents and protect their systems, data, and customers.

It is also important for organizations to educate their employees on cybersecurity best practices and awareness. Employee training should include information on how to identify and avoid phishing scams, the importance of using strong passwords, and the proper handling of sensitive information. Regular training can help to reduce the risk of human error and the likelihood of security incidents.

Another aspect to consider is the development of a cybersecurity incident response plan. This plan should outline the steps that the organization will take in the event of a security incident, including who is responsible for responding, the processes for containing and mitigating the incident, and the steps for reporting and documenting the incident. This plan helps organizations to be prepared in the event of a security incident and respond quickly and effectively.

It is also recommended for organizations to regularly perform security assessments and penetration testing.

Security assessments help organizations to identify vulnerabilities in their systems and data, while penetration testing simulates a real-world attack to determine the effectiveness of the organization's security controls. These assessments and tests provide valuable information to organizations about their security posture and can be used to improve their security measures.

In addition, organizations should consider implementing multi-factor authentication (MFA) for accessing sensitive systems and data. MFA requires users to provide multiple forms of authentication, such as a password and a one-time code sent to a mobile device, making it more difficult for unauthorized users to access sensitive information.

Finally, organizations should be mindful of their use of cloud services and ensure that their cloud service provider implements strong security measures. This includes encrypting data in transit and at rest, implementing access controls, and regularly monitoring the security of cloud systems and data. Organizations should also ensure that their cloud service provider has a well-defined incident response plan in place in the event of a security incident.

In conclusion, there are many steps that organizations can take to improve their cybersecurity posture. From implementing strong security measures and regularly monitoring systems, to developing a cybersecurity incident response plan and educating employees, organizations can reduce the risk of potential security incidents and protect their systems, data, and customers.

In today's digital world, cybersecurity is a critical concern for organizations of all sizes. With the increasing number of cyber attacks and data breaches, it is essential for organizations to have robust security measures in place to protect their systems, data, and customers. By taking proactive steps, organizations can minimize the risk of security incidents and ensure the safety of their sensitive information.

Continuous monitoring and regular updates of security measures are crucial for staying ahead of potential security threats. Organizations should also seek to educate their employees on the importance of cybersecurity and best practices for reducing the risk of human error.

Having a well-defined incident response plan in place is also essential in the event of a security incident. This plan outlines the steps that the organization will take to contain and mitigate the impact of a security breach, and can help organizations respond quickly and effectively.

Organizations should also consider implementing multi-factor authentication and regularly performing security assessments and penetration testing to identify vulnerabilities and improve their security posture. Additionally, it is important for organizations to ensure that their cloud service providers have strong security measures in place and a well-defined incident response plan.

In summary, there are many steps that organizations can take to improve their cybersecurity posture and protect their systems, data, and customers. By taking a proactive and comprehensive approach to cybersecurity, organizations can reduce the risk of security incidents and ensure the safety of their sensitive information.

when you cybersecruty vaiolates :

The punishment for someone who violates cybersecurity laws and regulations varies depending on the severity of the violation, the jurisdiction in which it occurred, and the type of data that was compromised. In general, violations of cybersecurity can result in civil penalties, fines, and imprisonment.

In the United States, for example, violating cybersecurity laws such as the Computer Fraud and Abuse Act, Electronic Communications Privacy Act, or the Health Insurance Portability and Accountability Act (HIPAA) can result in fines, imprisonment, and/or both. In some cases, organizations can also face lawsuits from customers whose personal information was compromised as a result of a security breach.

In other countries, such as the United Kingdom, violations of cybersecurity laws can result in criminal penalties, including imprisonment, fines, and/or both. Some countries have also enacted specific cybersecurity laws, such as the General Data Protection Regulation (GDPR) in the European Union, that outline specific penalties for data breaches and violations of privacy laws.

It is important to note that the punishment for violating cybersecurity laws and regulations can be severe and it is essential for individuals and organizations to be aware of their obligations and to take appropriate measures to protect sensitive data and systems. By taking proactive steps to improve their cybersecurity posture and stay informed about evolving threats, individuals and organizations can reduce the risk of security incidents and minimize the potential impact of a breach.

WannaCry ransomware attack: In May 2017, the WannaCry ransomware attack affected over 200,000 computers in 150 countries, causing widespread disruption and financial losses. The attack exploited vulnerabilities in outdated software and spread rapidly, encrypting users' files and demanding payment in exchange for the decryption key. The attackers behind the WannaCry attack have not been identified or charged, but if they had been caught, they could have faced charges under computer fraud laws and penalties such as imprisonment, fines, or both.

Capital One data breach: In 2019, a former software engineer was charged with hacking into the servers of Capital One Financial Corporation and stealing sensitive data belonging to over 100 million customers, including names, addresses, credit scores, and Social Security numbers. The defendant was sentenced to serve time in federal prison and pay a fine of $70,000. This case serves as an example of the severe consequences that individuals can face if they violate cybersecurity laws and steal sensitive data. The defendant's actions resulted in significant harm to Capital One and its customers, and the punishment imposed sends a strong message about the importance of protecting sensitive information and the consequences of violating cybersecurity laws.

In addition to civil and criminal penalties, individuals and organizations that violate cybersecurity laws may also face reputational damage, loss of trust from customers, and damage to their brand. This can have long-lasting impacts, especially for organizations that rely heavily on their reputation and customer trust for success.

In some cases, individuals and organizations may also face regulatory investigations and audits, which can be time-consuming and costly, even if no violations are found. This highlights the importance of being proactive in protecting sensitive data and ensuring compliance with cybersecurity laws and regulations.

Furthermore, organizations may also face legal claims from customers whose personal information was compromised in a breach. This highlights the need for organizations to have strong security measures in place and to take steps to minimize the risk of a security breach.

In conclusion, the consequences of violating cybersecurity laws and regulations can be severe and far-reaching. Individuals and organizations must be proactive in protecting sensitive data and ensuring compliance with relevant laws and regulations. By taking steps to improve their cybersecurity posture and being aware of evolving threats, individuals and organizations can minimize the risk of security incidents and reduce the potential impact of a breach.

Cybersecurity has become an increasingly important issue in todays digital age, as the number of cyber attacks continues to grow and the potential consequences of a breach become increasingly severe. In response to this growing threat, governments around the world have enacted a number of laws and regulations aimed at protecting sensitive information and improving cybersecurity. However, despite these efforts, individuals and organizations still face significant risks, and the consequences of violating cybersecurity laws can be severe. One of the main consequences of violating cybersecurity laws is the potential for criminal or civil penalties. This can include fines, imprisonment, or both, depending on the nature of the violation and the jurisdiction in which the individual or organization is located. For example, under the Computer Fraud and Abuse Act in the United States, individuals can face penalties of up to 20 years in prison and fines of up to $250,000 for unauthorized access to protected computers.

In addition to these criminal and civil penalties, individuals and organizations may also face reputational damage as a result of a security breach. This can be especially damaging for organizations that rely heavily on their reputation and customer trust for success. For example, if a financial institution is hacked and sensitive customer data is stolen, this could lead to a loss of trust and confidence among customers, which could have long-lasting impacts on the organizations financial stability and future success.

In some cases, individuals and organizations may also face regulatory investigations and audits as a result of a breach. This can be time-consuming and costly, even if no violations are found. This highlights the importance of being proactive in protecting sensitive data and ensuring compliance with cybersecurity laws and regulations.

Furthermore, organizations may also face legal claims from customers whose personal information was compromised in a breach. This highlights the need for organizations to have strong security measures in place and to take steps to minimize the risk of a security breach. This can include conducting regular security assessments, implementing strong access controls, and regularly updating software and systems to address known vulnerabilities.

In conclusion, the consequences of violating cybersecurity laws and regulations can be severe and far-reaching. Individuals and organizations must be proactive in protecting sensitive data and ensuring compliance with relevant laws and regulations. By taking steps to improve their cybersecurity posture and being aware of evolving threats, individuals and organizations can minimize the risk of security incidents and reduce the potential impact of a breach. In addition, it is important to foster a culture of continuous learning, as the threat landscape is constantly changing and new threats emerge regularly. By staying informed and up-to-date on the latest security trends and technologies, individuals and organizations can better protect themselves from cyber attacks and minimize the risk of violating cybersecurity laws.

Another aspect to consider when it comes to violating cybersecurity laws is the impact it can have on international relations and diplomacy. Cyberattacks and data breaches can often cross international borders, and the consequences of such incidents can be far-reaching and difficult to predict. For example, if a foreign entity is found to be responsible for a breach, this could lead to diplomatic tensions and could impact trade relations and other international agreements.

In some cases, violations of cybersecurity laws may also have implications for national security. For example, if state-sponsored actors are found to be responsible for a breach, this could raise serious concerns about the security of critical infrastructure and the ability of a country to defend itself against cyber attacks. As such, it is important for governments to take a proactive approach to cybersecurity and to work together with international partners to address this growing threat.

In addition to the legal and reputational consequences of violating cybersecurity laws, organizations must also consider the impact of a breach on their employees and customers. For example, if sensitive customer data is stolen, this could lead to identity theft and other financial crimes, which could have a profound impact on individuals lives. Similarly, if an employees personal information is compromised, this could lead to a loss of privacy and a sense of violation.

It is also worth mentioning the cost of remediation that follows a cyber attack. This can include the cost of notifying affected individuals, providing credit monitoring services, and making any necessary repairs to systems and software. In some cases, the cost of remediation can be significant and can have a lasting impact on an organizations finances and operations.

In conclusion, the consequences of violating cybersecurity laws and regulations can be severe and far-reaching. Organizations must take a proactive approach to protecting sensitive data and must stay informed about evolving threats and new technologies. By taking steps to improve their cybersecurity posture and being aware of the legal and regulatory landscape, organizations can reduce the risk of a breach and minimize the potential consequences if a breach does occur.

Cybersecurity refers to the practice of protecting internet-connected systems, including hardware, software, and data, from attack, damage, or unauthorized access. It encompasses a range of technologies, processes, and practices designed to secure networks, computers, and data from theft, damage, or unauthorized access.

Threats to cybersecurity come in various forms including viruses, malware, hacking, and phishing. To prevent these threats, individuals and organizations must implement strong cybersecurity measures, including firewalls, antivirus software, encryption, and secure passwords.

One of the biggest challenges in cybersecurity is keeping up with evolving threats. As technology continues to advance, new forms of cyberattacks are constantly emerging. It's essential that individuals and organizations regularly update their cybersecurity measures to stay ahead of these threats.

Another important aspect of cybersecurity is user education. End-users must be educated about safe online practices, including avoiding suspicious emails and downloading unknown software. They must also be taught how to recognize and respond to cyberattacks, such as reporting any suspected incidents to the appropriate authorities.

Organizations must also take proactive measures to secure their systems and data. This includes regularly backing up important data, monitoring network activity, and implementing access controls to prevent unauthorized users from accessing sensitive information.

In recent years, governments and businesses have increased their investment in cybersecurity. This has led to the development of new technologies and practices to help protect against cyberattacks. For example, machine learning and artificial intelligence (AI) algorithms are now being used to detect and prevent cyber threats in real-time.

However, the increasing reliance on technology has also created new vulnerabilities. For example, the growing use of cloud computing and internet of things (IoT) devices has expanded the attack surface for cyber criminals. This highlights the need for organizations to be proactive in their approach to cybersecurity and to continuously assess and update their security measures.

In conclusion, cybersecurity is a critical issue that affects individuals and organizations worldwide. To stay protected, it's essential to be proactive and to stay up to date on the latest threats and best practices for preventing cyberattacks. The combination of strong security measures, user education, and continuous assessment will help to ensure that individuals and organizations are protected against cyber threats.

THE END

www.ingramcontent.com/pod-product-compliance
Lightning Source LLC
LaVergne TN
LVHW091136180726
843490LV00008B/3001